W9-BNV-174

THE CIRCUS

SHIP

by
Chris Van Dusen
Author & Illustrator

Candlewick Press

Five miles off the coast of Maine
and slightly overdue,
a circus ship was steaming south
in fog as thick as stew.

On board were fifteen animals
who traveled to and fro.
The next day, it was Boston
for another circus show.

The captain, Mr. Carrington,
was honest and sincere.
He thought that they should drop the hook
and wait for things to clear.

But Mr. Paine, the circus boss,
was terribly demanding.
He stomped up to the helm,
where Captain Carrington was standing,

and screamed, "Don't stop! Keep going!
I've got a show to do!
Just get me down to Boston town
tomorrow, sir, by two!"

Then came a CRASH! An awful BASH!
Things flew into the air!
The ship had smashed into a ledge
that no one knew was there.

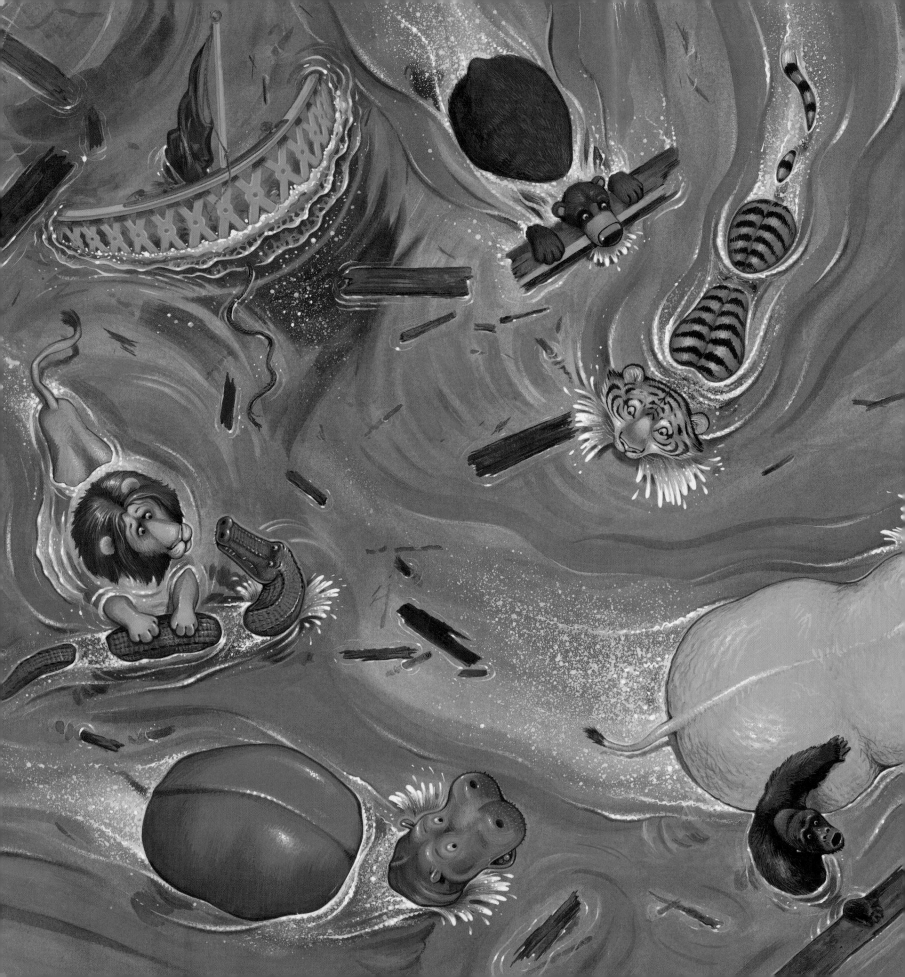

The shattered ship began to tip,
then sank without a sound.
The splashing, thrashing animals
swam round and round and round.

The captain said to Mr. Paine,
"Pray tell—what shall we do?
We can't just leave them here to drown—
we've got to save them too!"

"The animals?" yelled Mr. Paine.
"Why, sir, what are you, DAFT?
It's ME that you should rescue!
Pull me up into the raft!

"Now ferry me to safety, sir,
before I die of cold.
Don't question me!" barked Mr. Paine.
"Just do as you are told."

They pulled themselves up on the shore—
bedraggled, cold, and beat—
then staggered to the village
on weary, wobbly feet.

The people in the neighborhood
had just begun to rise,
and when they saw those animals,
they had to rub their eyes.

They thought they saw an elephant—
but wait, how could that be?
And what's that little monkey doing
in the cherry tree?

Mr. Hood was stacking wood
and nearly jumped a mile
when he found the alligator
sleeping on his pile!

And Mrs. Dottie Dailey,
who grew daisies by the bunch,
discovered that the zebra
had been eating them for lunch!

And Miss Fannie Feeney found—
according to the rumors—
the silly little circus monkey
swinging in her bloomers!

But everything changed quickly,
like the turning of the tide,
the night the Abbotts' shed caught fire
with Emma Rose inside!

From high above the Abbotts' farm,
the tiger saw the shed.
The sight of smoke and fire
triggered something in his head.

He'd jumped through flames a thousand times
back in his circus days,
so he ran past all the people,
and he leapt into the blaze!

Then everybody panicked—
"Help! Help! What can we do?"—
when from the raging fire,
something big burst into view.

It was the most amazing sight,
and everybody froze
when they saw the tiger
saving little Emma Rose!

The tiger's risky rescue
changed everybody's mind—
the animals weren't bothersome;
the animals were kind.

And so they lived together;
side by side they got along.
It didn't seem like anything
could possibly go wrong.

Then little Red, the messenger,
came running with the word.
Apparently a circus ship
had sunk, from what he'd heard.

"The animals are from that boat.
They swam in from the bay.
The greedy owner wants them back.
He'll be here any day!"

So the people called a meeting,
and they quickly hatched a plan:
No animal that came ashore
would sail off with that man.

The next day at the crack of dawn,
a ship was at the pier,
and up the lane marched Mr. Paine,
whose voice was loud and clear:

"I am the circus owner.
My ship sank in the murk.
I've come to find my animals
and put them back to work."

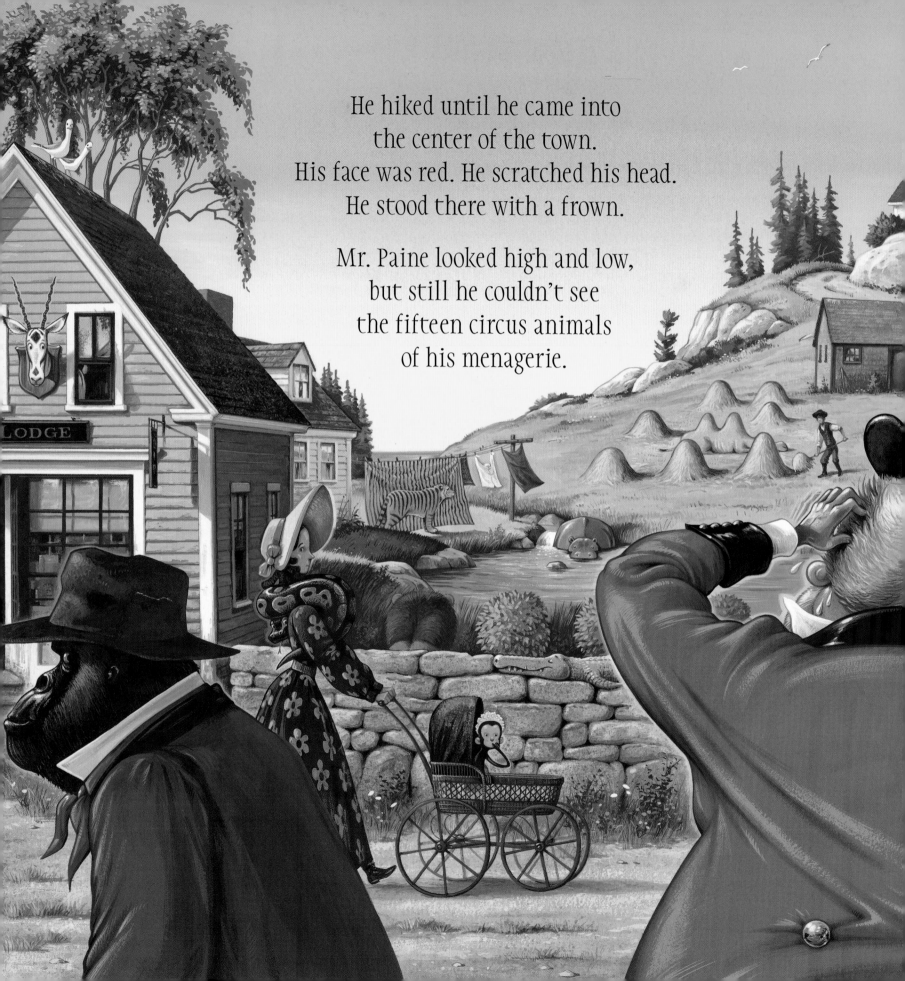

He hiked until he came into
the center of the town.
His face was red. He scratched his head.
He stood there with a frown.

Mr. Paine looked high and low,
but still he couldn't see
the fifteen circus animals
of his menagerie.

He ran around the alleyways.

He searched the village square.

He even checked a chicken coop—
his animals weren't there.

Mr. Paine was tuckered out.
His heavy chest was heaving.
Then little Red stepped up and said,
"I think your boat is leaving."

He ran off in a fit of rage.
His ship was leaving sight,
so he jumped into a rowboat,
and he rowed with all his might.

And from that day they like to say
their lives were free of "Paine."
It was a happy, peaceful place
upon that isle in Maine.

To my sons, Ethan and Tucker, and my wife, Lori, who make up my little island

AUTHOR'S NOTE

It may seem hard to believe, but the basic idea for *The Circus Ship* germinated from an actual event.

On October 25, 1836, the *Royal Tar,* a side-wheel steamer, was sailing from St. John, New Brunswick, to Portland, Maine. On board were 103 passengers and a complete circus, including an elephant, two lions, a tiger, a leopard, six horses, two camels, a gnu, two pelicans, and a collection of exotic serpents and birds, as well as a full band.

With such unusual cargo, the journey started out in a festive mood. The circus band played and people cheered as the animals were paraded around the deck for exercise. But when the *Royal Tar* ran into a gale off the island of Vinalhaven, disaster struck. Through a series of unfortunate miscommunications, the boiler overheated and the ship went up in flames. The scene turned to panic and chaos as people and animals leaped from the burning vessel. Though several people were saved, many lost their lives, and it's believed that most of the animals perished. There are rumors, however, that the elephant (named Mogul) survived the disaster by swimming to nearby Brimstone Island. Later, unidentified leg bones from a large land animal were discovered there. And on Crotch Island, off Stonington, people reported seeing exotic serpents for many years after the tragic wreck of the *Royal Tar.*

In writing *The Circus Ship,* it was never my goal to accurately retell the story of the *Royal Tar.* Although it is a fascinating slice of Maine history, it is also terrifying and traumatic. Instead, I changed the details to create a new adventure for children that hopefully still captures the spirit of the *Royal Tar.*

ACKNOWLEDGMENTS

Thanks to the Penobscot Marine Museum, the Camden History Center, the Vinalhaven Historical Society, and my mom and dad for help with historical references. Thanks also to *Down East* magazine, where I first read about the *Royal Tar;* Loretta Krupinski; Kelly Paul Briggs; fellow authors and illustrators who generously fed me materials; my editor, Joan Powers, for fine-tuning my story; and art director Ann Stott for making it all beautiful. Finally, a special thank-you to my friend Emma Rose for letting me borrow her name.

Copyright © 2009 by Chris Van Dusen. All rights reserved. No part of this book may be reproduced, transmitted, or stored in an information retrieval system in any form or by any means, graphic, electronic, or mechanical, including photocopying, taping, and recording, without prior written permission from the publisher. First paperback edition 2015. Library of Congress Cataloging-in-Publication Data is available. Library of Congress Catalog Card Number 2008938402. ISBN 978-0-7636-3090-4 (hardcover). ISBN 978-0-7636-5592-1 (paperback). This book was typeset in Integrity JY Lining. The illustrations were done in gouache. Candlewick Press, 99 Dover Street, Somerville, Massachusetts 02144. visit us at www.candlewick.com. Printed in Humen, Dongguan, China. 15 16 17 18 19 SCP 10 9 8 7 6 5 4 3 2